THE MAMMOTH BOOK OF
ILLUSTRATED
EROTIC WOMEN

THE MAMMOTH BOOK OF
ILLUSTRATED
EROTIC WOMEN

Edited by Maxim Jakubowski

CARROLL & GRAF PUBLISHERS

New York

Carroll & Graf Publishers
An imprint of Avalon Publishing Group, Inc.
245 W. 17th Street
New York
NY 10011-5300
www.carrollandgraf.com

AVALON
publishing group incorporated

First published in the UK in 2005 by Robinson,
an imprint of Constable & Robinson Ltd

First Carroll & Graf edition 2005

ISBN 0-7867-1602-9

Design and layout by Talking Design
Printed and bound in Singapore

PHOTOGRAPH CREDITS

Title page: Heather Corinna
Imprint page: Roger Gaess
Contents page: Ivana Ford
Page 8: Pascal Baetens; page 9: Konstantin Korneshov; page 10: René Whitfield;
page 11: Juergen Specht

CONTENTS

HENRIK AGELBY	12	
TAMI AMIT	18	
SARYN ANGEL	24	
PASCAL BAETENS	30	
PHILIPPE BAUD	36	
LAURENT BENAIM	42	
ERIC BOUTILIER BROWN	48	
JENS BRÜGGEMANN	54	
DIDIER CARRÉ	60	
JESÚS COLL	66	
CHRIS COLLIER	72	
GRANT COLLIER	78	
HEATHER CORINNA	84	
MIKE CRAWLEY	90	
KATE CYMMER	96	
RENÉ DE HAAN	102	
EMMA DELVES-BROUGHTON		
	108	
JAEDA DEWALT	114	
MARK FISHER	120	
IVANA FORD	126	
JODY FROST	132	
ROGER GAESS	138	
PERRY GALLAGHER	144	
CHARLES GATEWOOD	150	
STEVE DIET GOEDDE	156	
GERO GRÖSCHEL	162	

AARON HAWKS	168	
PETTER HEGRE	174	
PAUL HERNANDEZ	180	
BENJAMIN HOFFMAN	186	
R C HÖRSCH	192	
KEVIN HUNDSNURSCHER	198	
NAD IKSODAS	204	
JIMON	210	
PATRICK KAAS	216	
KONSTANTIN KORNESHOV		
	222	
MARTIN KRAKE	228	
CHAS RAY KRIDER	234	
ERIC KROLL	240	
BORYS KURYLO	246	
MANUEL LAVAL	252	
TRACY LEE	258	
DENNIS LETBETTER	264	
THERESA LO SCHIAVO	270	
JOZSEF LOVASZ	276	
MAELWYS	282	
JEFFREY MCALLISTER	288	
STEPHEN MCCLURE	294	
ANDY METAL	300	
CARINA MEYER-BROICHER		
	306	
LIEVEN MICHIELS	312	
CRAIG MOREY	318	
HANS-PETER MUFF	324	

DAVE NAZ	330
KIM NIELSEN	336
MICHAEL PECHA	342
ZBIGNIEW RESZKA	348
GABRIELE RIGON	354
JUAN CARLOS RIVAS	360
KATI RUDLOVA	366
JOHN RUNNING	372
RAECHEL RUNNING	378
WILL SANTILLO	384
IVAN SCHEERS	390
MATT SCHNEIDER	396
IAN SCRIVENER	402
MICHELE SERCHUK	408
JUERGEN SPECHT	414
JOERN STUBBE	420
MARCO TENAGLIA	426
CARSTEN TSCHACH	432
MIKKEL URUP	438
LARRY UTLEY	444
MARIANO VARGAS	450
KIM WESTON	456
RENE WHITFIELD	462
MICHAEL WILCE	468
JAMES WILLIAMS	474

INTRODUCTION

It is true that the erotic is often in the eye of the beholder, and that standards and attitudes differ, but the beauty of women is never in doubt. Their bodies, the splendour of their nudity, their eyes, the ever-changing curves that define them, the flick of their hair, the geography of their breasts, the mystery of their sex – these are universal and everlasting. An image of a naked woman, any woman, is not limited to

body shape and contours – it is all of her, a reflection of her personality in the way she looks under the sometimes harsh and uncompromising view of the photographer's lens, and no two women are the same. Every woman reveals to the world yet another of the billion facets of femininity. Every photograph renews our inspiration and our faith in the eternal feminine.

In this volume there are hundreds of absolutely splendid photographs of women, nude and partly nude, in shadow and in light, and for me, as editor and compiler of the book, every single one is profoundly erotic. For you, the anonymous viewer who has picked up this book, it is inevitable that some will arouse you, some will intrigue you, some will you leave you almost indifferent, some might even shock you and others might well puzzle you. We each bring a different perspective to our voyeurism, a perspective born of our individual experiences and background, from our past struggles with lust, desire and the essence of beauty. But I sincerely believe that every image in these pages will strike a chord with someone.

This collection of photographs is a unique celebration
of the female human form as seen through the eyes
and camera of 78 different photographers from all over
the world. The initial volume in the series, *The
Mammoth Book of Erotic Photography* (or, as it was
entitled in the USA, *The Mammoth Book of Illustrated
Erotica*) has proven to be a major success, with
wonderful reviews and a score of reprints and foreign
language editions. As you will see in the following
pages, the first volume only dipped into the well of
talent practising the art of nude photography.
In this new volume, 18 of the photographers who
appeared in the first book make a welcome return,
with new, innovative images, and in many cases now
working in colour instead of only black and white, and

I am grateful for their trust and continued collaboration. I have also
cast the net wider, and am pleased to bring on board several of my
favourite photographers who were not available last time around, as
well as taking the opportunity to introduce impressive new talents.

I'm also very pleased to be able to feature many more female
photographers of the nude (some of whom, intriguingly, practise the
art of self portraiture), giving us a chance to see how gender can subtly
influence ways of looking at the human body. We also have a father
and daughter, both with the same passion for fine art photography; a
photographer who also appears as a model in two other portfolios; the
grandson of the famed American photographer Edward Weston; a mix
of professional and amateur photographers; and contributions from the

UK, the USA, Spain, Belgium, Denmark, Germany, Austria, Russia, Argentina, France, Israel, Italy, Poland, Norway, Switzerland, Japan, Australia, Canada, Slovakia and The Netherlands. How could one be more international?

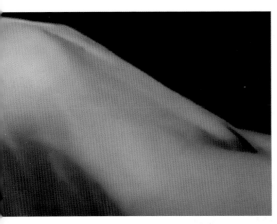

I don't think I will ever tire of the sight of women in their glorious nudity, and so many of the images I've had the privilege to select for this book (from amongst literally tens of thousands viewed and submitted) speak to me in the language of eroticism – they tell me a story. Every image is tantalising, fascinating, seductive, daring, mysterious – as are the women who so openly display their incomparable beauty with such innocence and wanton splendour. We are blessed by their daring.

I owe a vote of thanks to several people without whom this book would not have come about: to Nick Robinson, publisher extraordinaire, who suggested that I take a temporary detour from prose into photography, a courageous proposal to someone who, ironically, has almost never taken a photograph in his whole life (although I never revealed that fact to Nick!); to Marilyn Jaye-Lewis, who was my co-conspirator on the first volume but who could not come on board this time, due to writing commitments; to Eric Kroll and Anna Maria Staiano, who suggested many fine photographers that I should approach; and, last but not least, to Dolores, who generously indulged me and allowed me to look at the bodies of scores of other women and barely batted an eyelid.

Feast your eyes and your senses with joyful abandon.

Maxim Jakubowski

HENRIK AGELBY

Henrik Agelby was born in
1963 in Copenhagen. Since
1983 he has worked full-time
in the insurance business. He
took up photography in 1990,
and in 1992 several of his
erotic images were selected for
an exhibition at Copenhagen's
Erotic Museum. He has since
worked on a freelance basis for
various magazines all over the
world. In 2004, his own book
of black and white
photography, entitled *Passion*,
was published in Denmark.

www.agelby.dk

TAMI AMIT

Tami Amit was born in Tel Aviv,
Israel, in 1972. She now works
and lives in Paris. She attended
the Parsons School of Design in
Paris and New York between
1994 and 1997 and obtained a
BFA. She has worked as assistant
to several major photographers,
has exhibited in Israel, the
Netherlands, Belgium and Paris,
and has contributed to scores of
magazines. She published a
book of her own photographs
entitled *Petrified Forest*.

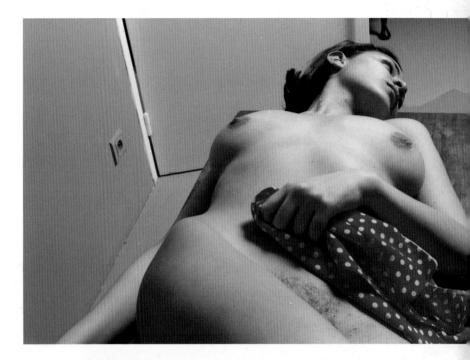

SARYN ANGEL

Saryn Angel has been a photographer for over 15 years, focusing mostly on fetish and erotica for the past six years. She works out of her home in Los Angeles, California, photographing women of all varieties, both amateur and professional models, found through the Internet and from the Los Angeles club scene. Saryn's work has been published in *Tattoo, Savage, Gothic Beauty* and *DDI* (*Dominatrix Directory International*), and has been shown in galleries throughout the Los Angeles area.

www.sarynangel.com

PASCAL BAETENS

Pascal Baetens was born in Leuven, Belgium, in 1963. After gaining degrees in Law and Politics and Social Sciences, he studied photography in Greece, the USA and Belgium. He soon established himself as a professional photographer with his work in fashion, reportage and travel. His work has often been published and exhibited, and has been featured in some of the leading books on modern photography. His books include *The Fragile Touch* (1999), *Heavenly Girls* (2001), *Allegro Sensibile* (2002) and *The Art Of Nude Photography* (2003). He lives in Belgium and works from his studio in Kessel-Lo.

www.pascalbaetens.com

PHILIPPE BAUD

Philippe Baud is a professional photographer living in Canada. His lifelong photographic interests include capturing the beauty of natural landscapes, heritage architecture and various forms of figure photography. His current work includes an exploration of pattern and design features in the natural world. His work has been shown in numerous Canadian galleries and published in a number of magazines and books, including *The Mammoth Book of Erotic Photography*. A regular contributor to websites such as photoselection.com, met-art.com and domai.com, Philippe is the owner and

webmaster of artisticnudegirls.com, showcasing his figure photography and the work of other professional photographers.

www.philippebaud.com

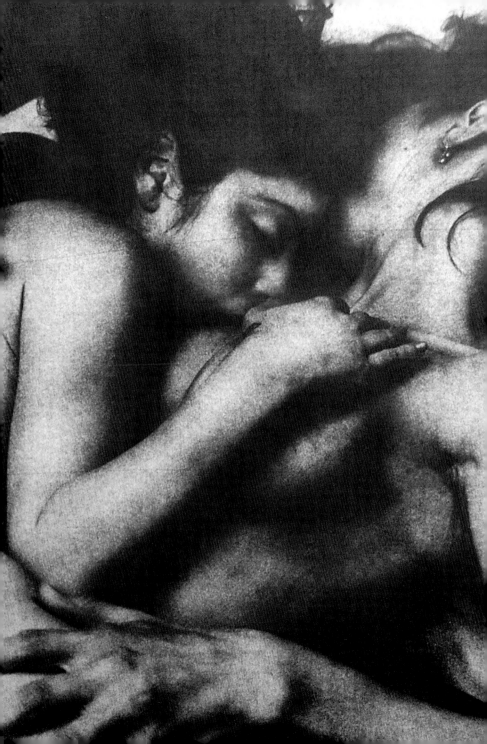

LAURENT BENAIM

Laurent Benaim was born in Paris, France, in 1965. Following a career as a commercial photographer, he spent the last ten years working as a creative photographer.

He says, 'My photographic approach is born from an intense curiosity to seize nudity, to reveal movement and a sense of disturbance, and to uncover the emotional intimacy within the bodies of others. My models come from all over, each leaving behind with me a bit of themselves. And out of these gifts, I conjure up images.' Benaim puts in considerable effort in the lab to achieve the desired texture in his pictures. His book *Corpus Delicti* appeared in 2002.

www.laurentbenaim.com

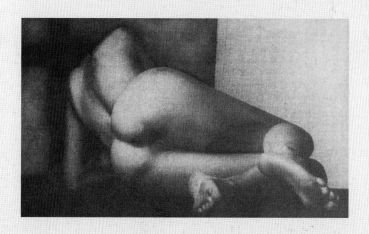

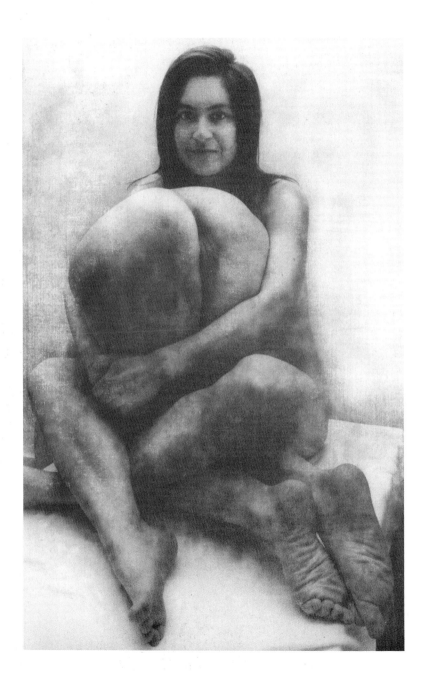

ERIC BOUTILIER BROWN

Canadian photographer Eric
Boutilier-Brown was interested
in the nude long before he
discovered photography. He
vividly remembers seeing
Michelangelo's *David and the
Dying Slaves* at the age of ten,
an experience that shaped his
appreciation for the human
figure. Eric went to Art
College intending to study
sculpture, but photography
won him over. He does no
commercial work, preferring to
focus on exploring his personal
creative vision, striving to show
the marvellous in the
commonplace and offering the
viewer a new sensuous and
aesthetic insight into
something undeniably familiar.

www.evolvingbeauty.com

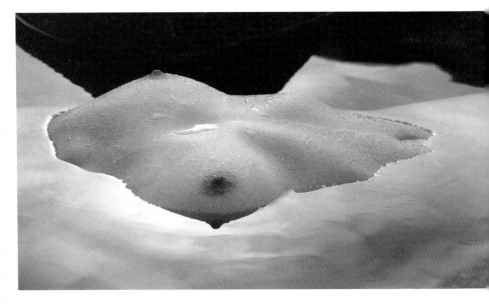

JENS BRÜGGEMANN

Jens Brüggemann was born in 1968. He studied economics, graduating in 1998, and has since worked as a freelance photographic designer in the fields of fashion, beauty, people, erotic fine arts and stills. His studio is in Düsseldorf. Most of his artistic nudes have been published in his books *Schwarzweiss Aktfotografie* (1998), *Erotic Moments* (2000), *Erotic Acts* (2000), *Passion* (2001), *Best Of Black And White* (2002) and *Best Of Color* (2004). He works almost exclusively with medium–format cameras (Rolleiflex 6008 Integral and 6008 AF, Zeiss and Schneider lenses).

www.jensbrueggemann.de

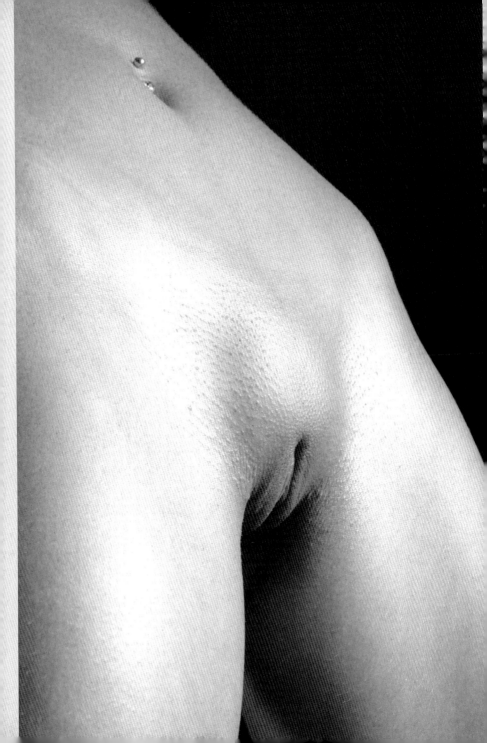

DIDIER CARRÉ

Didier Carré lives in Paris, France, close to the Pigalle neighbourhood where he spent his childhood. Following classical and photographic studies, he was the assistant to the Paris National Opera's photographer, and then managed a black and white photographic laboratory until his passion for women led him to devote all his time to his art. His images, at once both classical and insolent, present a world where the models appear to be sweet or indecent depending on their mood, proud to show themselves in a way you seldom see anywhere else.

www.gallerycarre.com

Jesús Coll

An all-round professional photographer, Spanish-born Jesús Coll has tackled subjects as diverse and opposed as fast, noisy race cars to quiet natural landscapes, tiny jewels to large studio performances, ordinary, everyday objects to the unique and the sophisticated. Every situation has brought him the chance to learn something new, as much from the mistakes as the successes. His passion is black and white photography, and he tries out new ideas with every model session. A true 'multimedia man', Jesús is as comfortable with the computer as he is with the camera.

www.jesuscoll.com/erotic

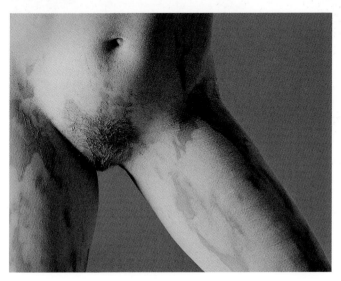

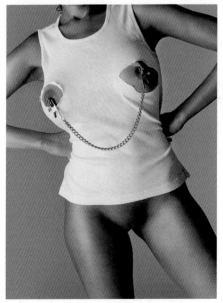

CHRIS COLLIER

The small team at sharkinfestedwaters has always believed that erotic photography should never be faked, and they believe that friends and lovers are far more beautiful and inspiring than any model from a catalogue agency. They don't work agency hours anyway. 'When, after 15 years, I left a career in music journalism,' says Chris, 'I vowed to concentrate on taking snaps that could get us into trouble. The erotic can be the everyday. It can be bright and loud and full of life and mischief. It's punk rock pornography, and that's all we've ever tried to do.'

www.sharkinfestedwaters.net

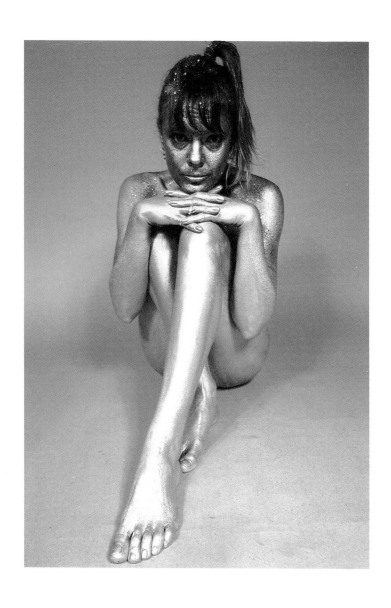

GRANT COLLIER

Grant Collier is a life-long resident of Denver, Colorado. He has been working as a professional photographer and writer since 1996 and is the author of the acclaimed books *Colorado: Yesterday & Today* and *Colorado: Moments in Time*. The artistic nude images shown here are part of a work-in-progress entitled *Collier Nudes*.

In addition to his more traditional images, this book will feature some of Grant's unique and enigmatic digital imagery.
His fine art nudes have also been published in the UK in *The Special Reserve Collection* and *Jade Magazine*.

www.gcollier.com/nudes

HEATHER CORINNA

With her photography, Heather Corinna seeks to explore and examine themes of sexual self-identity and female sexuality, gender, sexual politics, beauty ideals and both the balance and imbalance of nature and technology. She currently lives and works in Minneapolis, Minnesota, and has been working full-time in woman-centred visual and textual art and sexuality for the last six years. Heather is the founder and editor of the Internet's first sexual arts and information site for women, *Scarlet Letters*, and her short stories have appeared in Maxim Jakubowski's *Mammoth Book of Erotica* series on various occasions.

www.heathercorinna.com

MIKE CRAWLEY

Considered one of the UK's leading erotic photographers, Mike Crawley was born in Kent and now lives in Hertfordshire. His interest in photographing beautiful women began when he attended photography evening classes in 1988. Since then he has gained several distinctions, including a Fellowship of the Royal Photographic Society, and has evolved his own inimitable style. Mike has exhibited his work in England and Europe, and has had many images and articles published in various magazines and books, including the first *Mammoth Book of Erotic Photography* and his own highly successful book, *Photographing the Nude.*

www.photofrenetic.com

KATE CYMMER

Kate Cymmer was born in Lodz, Poland, in 1982 and has lived in Göttingen since 1987. During her final school year, in 2002, she began experimenting intensively with photography, and her initial works involved themes with people and nudes, and nude studies have since become the major element in her photographic activities. In 2004, she won second prize in the erotic-bodyscapes section of *Photographie* magazine's contest. Kate manages to maintain her own soft, feminine style while negotiating the difficult border between artistic photography and simply parading bare skin – the total human being is always the most important element in her work.

www.sinnliche-welten.de

RENÉ DE HAAN

René De Haan was born in
Utrecht in the Netherlands in
1960. Self-taught, he bought
his first camera in 1982, and
began working as a freelance
photographer in 1988.
Introduced to the Dutch
edition of *Playboy* by a model,
his work has also been
published in *Viva* and *Men's
Health*, as well as in *Black &
White* and *Snoecks*, and he has
contributed to several books.
Most of his photographs are
taken with his old 500 C/M
Hasselblad, and he prefers black
and white to colour. He prefers
location to studio work, and
aims to capture the beauty and
'power' of women.

www.renedehaan.com

Emma Delves-Broughton

Emma Delves-Broughton lives in Bath, England, and works within the world of portraiture, fetish, fashion and beauty. She originally specialised in black and white photography, but is now equally at home with colour. Attention to detail is very important to her, which stems from her experience as a make-up artist and stylist. Most of her subjects are women. Emma has a particular empathy with other women, allowing them to feel relaxed and to enjoy themselves in front of the camera. Emma's work has appeared in a variety of magazines and books, and her first book is entitled *Kinky Couture*.

www.emmadelvesbroughton.com

Jaeda DeWalt

Jaeda DeWalt is a self-taught artist residing in Seattle, Washington. She has produced cover art for books, playbills and collective fine art books, and has had several exhibits of her work in New York, including the Hofstra Museum. After doing a self-portrait for the cover of her book *Haunting Hands* (1996), she fell in love with photography and has developed it into a full-time passion and career. In her work she expresses the sensual in all its colours, textures and feelings, as well as exposing the darker side. In self-portraiture she finds she can express herself freely and without boundaries.

www.jaedasfineart.com

MARK FISHER

Mark Fisher was born in London in 1961 and has been active in photography for more than 25 years. In addition to his nude and portrait work, he also loves to photograph landscapes and nature. Mark's approach to photographing the nude can be summed up in one word: natural. Using only natural light, he strives to capture the personality of the subject, to create a nude portrait rather than an impersonal figure study. Over the past 15 years, Mark has travelled widely, but he now divides his time between England, Argentina and Western Australia.

www.marchino.com

IVANA FORD

Ivana Ford was born and raised
in Southern California's Inland
Empire. She is primarily self-
taught in photography, and a
friend once commented that
he felt uneasy when he
watched her work. He was
formally trained in
photography and found her
methods to be uncomfortably
unorthodox. It was one of the
best compliments she had ever
received. In the late 80s and
early 90s she documented the
Los Angeles underground
techno-house scene. For her,
the unpredictability of the
locations and lighting
conditions, along with the
spontaneity of the dancers,
provided the perfect mix of
sexual energy and mesmerising
drama.

www.ivanaford.com
www.vixenobscura.com
www.powerdivas.com

JODY FROST

Jody Frost began modelling 20 years ago. From there she formed her own vision and ideas of what she wanted to see in an image and began experimenting in self-portraiture. She eventually moved on to shooting models, and from fine art nude studies for gallery shows to hardcore erotica for websites. She now finds herself most comfortable shooting more refined imagery that does not degrade but celebrates the feminine (and male) principle. Her photos have been shown in numerous galleries in New Mexico, Texas and New York and she is a regular contributor to *Cupido*. She lives in California.

www.frostfoto.com

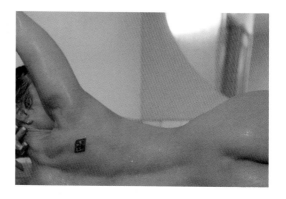

ROGER GAESS

Roger Gaess is a New York fine art photographer and photojournalist, with a special interest in Middle Eastern affairs. He also does dance, portrait and travel work. His images have appeared in a variety of published venues, including *Skin Two* and poster work for the Whitney Museum of American Art.

He is currently pursuing projects related to London railway ambience and the demise of eastern US factory towns. A fascination with the underbelly of life in all its wondrous forms is at the core of his photographic interests.

aqaba9@aol.com

PERRY GALLAGHER

The photography of Perry Gallagher is a celebration of women. His images show an intimacy and trust rarely captured. He is a master of available light, only using artificial light when necessary.

While his commercial work continues to grow, Perry remains faithful to his passion – erotic art. He is based in Los Angeles, California.

www.PerryGallagher.com

CHARLES GATEWOOD

Charles Gatewood is the
Walker Evans of the sexual
revolution. For more than 30
years his photographs have
probed the darkest corners of
New York and San Francisco's
erogenous zones. A schooled
anthropologist, he is naturally
curious about aberrant
cultures; a non-conformist
himself, he is always willing to
'join the dance', the better to
understand his subjects. 'Are
there still areas of the
behavioural map marked
"unknown"?' he asks. 'If so,
book my passage at once.' His
career retrospective book,
Badlands, appeared in 2000 and
is indispensable to all erotic
bookshelves.

www.charlesgatewood.com

STEVE DIET GOEDDE

Steve Diet Goedde is a Los
Angeles-based self-taught
erotic photographer who has
made himself a name by going
against the traditional clichés of
erotic photography. While most
others explore nude landscapes,
Goedde prefers to survey the
sensual appeal of fetishism.
Lovingly documenting such
textures as latex, PVC and
leather, he manages to remind
us that there are people under
the clothing. He refuses to
pursue photography
commercially and only works
on his own terms. His
retrospective books, *The Beauty
of Fetish* and *The Beauty of
Fetish vol 2*, are major
publications in the field.

www.stevedg.com

GERO GRÖSCHEL

Gero Gröschel was born in 1972 and lives in Germany. During his study of industrial design he discovered professional photography and spent most of his time in the photo design laboratory. After his studies, he decided to work as a freelance in the fields of graphics and photography. His main subject is people photography, ranging from business and glamour to pin-up and nude photography, and each composition is meticulously planned, with nothing left to chance. In addition to his work as a photographer, he holds a lectureship in Graphics and New Media at a private college in Stuttgart.

www.geroart.com

Aaron Hawks

Growing up in Seattle, Washington, Aaron Hawks began to pursue the naked body from the moment he first picked up a camera in 1990. Following the local scene, he soon found himself photographing strippers, artists and other eager exhibitionists. In 1998 he moved to San Francisco, where he began collaborating with Chuck Duke on several small films, and the experience gave him a new respect for image making. Aaron has become ever more aware of the relationship between the subject and the environment, and he has recently begun building his own photographic sets.

www.aaronhawks.net

PETTER HEGRE

Norwegian photographer
Petter Hegre worked as an
assistant to Richard Avedon
and then studied at the Brooks
Institute of Photography in
Santa Barbara, California. His
first book, *My Wife*, came about
after he took over 6,000
photos of his wife in six years,
and the book won the Erotic
Award for best photographer.
He has since published several
further books, including *Luba*,
and his work has been the
subject of a number of major
exhibitions. He has now
launched his own magazine,
Hegre, and he lives in Portugal.

www.petter-hegre.net

PAUL HERNANDEZ

Paul Hernandez began his career as a rock band photographer in Seattle, Washington, during the days of grunge music. He then moved on to fashion and fine art work, while living and travelling throughout the United States and Europe, exploring and developing his unique style. His interest in figure work began with a new-found respect for the masters of the past, such as Julia Margaret Cameron, Stieglitz and Robert Demachy. Their photographs, he feels, have soul and integrity and represent the history of this art form, which he feels obliged to keep alive.

www.paulhernandez-photography.com

BENJAMIN HOFFMAN

Benjamin Hoffman is based in Los Angeles, California, where he shares a studio with his cat, Midnight. Most of his work has been in fetish photography, an area in which he finds that black and white photography has a timeless quality. He believes this is a world that demands mystery, for it is a world often kept secret. It is a place that many people think of as smudgy and dark, but one that he perceives as quite beautiful. At times, his own shadow can be seen in the images, making this his most personal photography.

www.benjaminhoffman.com

R.C. HÖRSCH

R C Hörsch has followed a
life of dissipation as an artist,
film maker, composer, writer,
drug smuggler and sometime
sociopath, and he has spent
years in exile in New Zealand
and Australia. He made his
name with 60s magazine
layouts that juxtaposed high-
fashion models with skid row
backgrounds. Following
pioneering work for the
Children's Television
Workshops, he produced
several low-budget films and,
since 1993, ground-breaking
erotic documentaries. His
two-volume retrospective
book *Eroto* is a major
landmark on the scene, as is
his film *Slave*. He lives in
Pennsylvania.

www.eroto.com

KEVIN HUNDSNURSCHER

Kevin Hundsnurscher is from the Seattle area, where he takes publicly candid pictures of models, friends and bands, as well as doing more conceptualised shoots in semi-public locations. The subjects in his pictures are both professional models and personal friends. He is driven to create images that feature people completely transformed or in incongruous situations. Since all of his work is done outside the studio, every photo has its own story, and he tries to communicate this story through the picture, hoping that the viewer's experience of his work is as rewarding as it was for him to capture.

Kevin_h7@hotmail.com

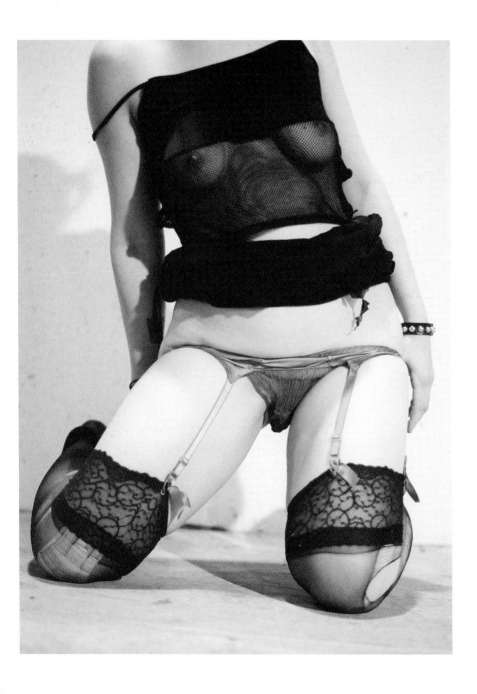

NAD IKSODAS

'When I see the light fall across the female form, I want others to see the beauty in the shape, in the play of light, in the way the model expresses herself. When I see a look, an expression, eyes that melt my soul, it needs to be shared. The model is my partner in the creative process. I have the greatest respect for the models I have been fortunate enough to work with. Fully clothed, barely covered or completely nude, they possess self-confidence, a belief in self and a desire that I can only begin to imagine from my side of the camera.'

www.nad-iksodas.com

JIMON

Jimon was born and raised in a religious Jewish family in Iran. After graduating, he moved to Europe and lived in Austria briefly before following his dream to move to Los Angeles, where he has been ever since. He acquired a Bachelors degree in engineering, which he pursued as a career until his passion for photography compelled him to change paths. Jimon explores various visual stimuli, from landscapes and documentary to whatever confronts his lens. Photographing friends, he discovered 'the way that soft light wraps and flows across the female form like a flawless erotic landscape', and there was no turning back.

www.Studiojimon.com

PATRICK KAAS

Patrick Kaas has his studio in Eindhoven, the Netherlands, where he was born and still lives and works. While studying chemical engineering and chemistry, he became interested in photography and acquired his first camera and some second-hand darkroom equipment. After researching the technical aspects of photography, he joined the student photography club at the Dekate Mouse University, and he quickly focused his interest on nude photography. In 2000, after completing his studies, he started his own company. Patrick mainly works on exhibitions and publishes widely, including in the Dutch edition of *Playboy*.

www.pk-foto.nl

KONSTANTIN KORNESHOV

Konstantin Korneshov is a freelance Russian photographer. He studied at the faculty of journalism of Moscow State University, which led him first into advertising and then – to his great satisfaction – into artistic photography. Konstantin takes as his starting point the texture of erotic photography of the late 19th and early 20th century. From here he has developed his own highly personal technique of composite black and white photography, toning and manual coloration to create a unique juxtaposition of style and content.

www.korneshov.ru

MARTIN KRAKE

Martin Krake took up nude photography in 1989 at the age of 19, after dealing with landscapes and still lifes for several years. Encouraged by the results, he worked alone to improve his style and technical skills without any formal training, and he can claim to be a truly self-made photographer. In 1995 he moved away from black and white photography and changed to a more pin-up style, opening the door to commercial work and a career as a fully professional nude photographer. In the commercial arena, Martin works under the name of Victor Lindenborn. He lives in Vienna, Austria.

www.victorlindenborn.com

CHAS RAY KRIDER

Based in Columbus, Ohio, Chas Ray Krider has attained a considerable reputation for his ambiguous and fascinating work in the field of fetish glamour. His book *Motel Fetish* (2002) presents some striking noir images reminiscent of David Lynch at his most troubling, even though one can also detect a strong and impish sense of humour underlying the sexy and evocative images of damsels in distress (or are they femmes fatales in bondage?). Many of the photos first appeared in *Pure* magazine. He is also responsible for the cover of Maxim Jakubowski's novel *Kiss Me Sadly*.

www.motelfetish.com

ERIC KROLL

Eric Kroll graduated from the University of Colorado in 1969. He founded and ran the One Loose Eye Gallery of Photography in Taos, New Mexico, from 1969 to 1971, and then moved to New York, where he worked as a photojournalist for the *New York Times*, *Der Spiegel*, *Vogue* and others, and taught photography at Hunter College. His work has since appeared in all the major magazines in the field. He now lives in San Francisco. His books include *Fetish Girls*, *Eric Kroll's Beauty Parade* and the two volumes of *The Transformation Of Gwen*.

www.erickroll.com

BORYS KURYLO

Borys S. Kurylo was born in 1960 in the small town of Hünfeld, in Germany. Even as a very young boy, his ambition was to become 'a photographer'. However, he first studied business computer studies and only after completing his studies did he begin to develop systematically his love for photography, specialising in portrait and nude photography. In the mid-90s he focused his attention on digital image processing, and he now combines his knowledge of computers with his skill as a photographer. His work has been shown in several exhibitions and successfully published in books.

www.kurylo.de

MANUEL LAVAL

Manuel Laval was born in
1952 in Germany and studied
electrical engineering. He
worked for many years as a
supervising sound designer on
a wide variety of film projects,
and has lectured on movie
language and sound. He is a
self-taught photographer who
also works in video and other
visual media. His first photo
exhibition was in 1993, and he
has since been the subject of
numerous exhibitions and been
published widely in books and
magazines.

www.manuel-laval.de

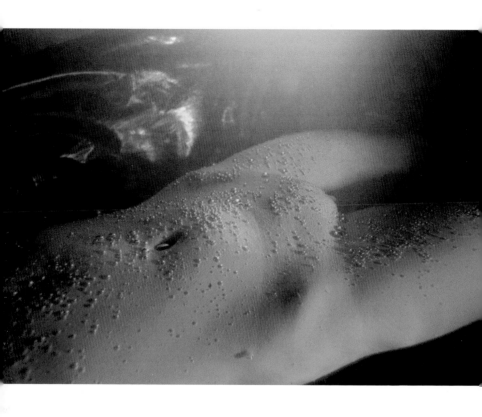

TRACY LEE

For 15 years, Tracy Lee's erotica photography has featured a single model – herself. Her portfolio consequently reflects her evolving perspective on the art from both sides of the camera. One of the original online journalists, she has been profiled in *The Village Voice* and *Yahoo: Internet Life*, among other publications. Her work appeared in the books *Torn Shapes of Desire: Internet Erotica* (1996) and *Naked Women: The Female Nude in Photography from 1850 to the Present Day* (2001). The recent photographs on these pages were taken around Washington, D.C., where she resides with her family and dogs.

www.angstbabe.com

DENNIS LETBETTER

Dennis Letbetter is a San Francisco-based photographer who has been widely exhibited and published. His work in a variety of genres can be seen in several books dedicated to his own work as well as collaborative projects. His book *Jane* features some of his nude work and follows one model posing in every room of an empty 19th-century Victorian home, all shot on the same day. Most recently, Dennis has been concentrating on panoramic cityscapes in the US, Russia, Europe and Japan.

www.studioletbetter.com

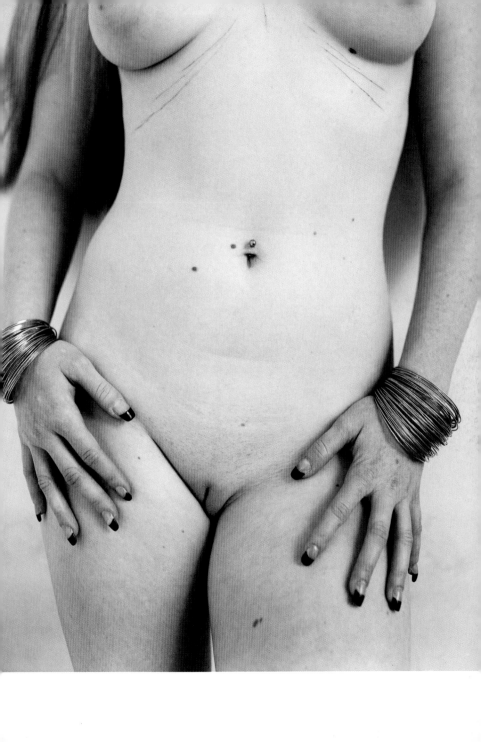

THERESA LOSCHIAVO

For Theresa LoSchiavo, photography is all about capturing a moment. Her images illustrate the sensual side of women, while revealing the beauty within, and she does so with a rare touch of class that has brought compliments flooding into her website from all around the world. She has a talent for discovering the humanity within people, a skill that she developed while growing up in New York. When Theresa moved to Washington she founded her own business photographing horses and, eventually, weddings – which ultimately led to her signature speciality of photographing women.

www.museme.com

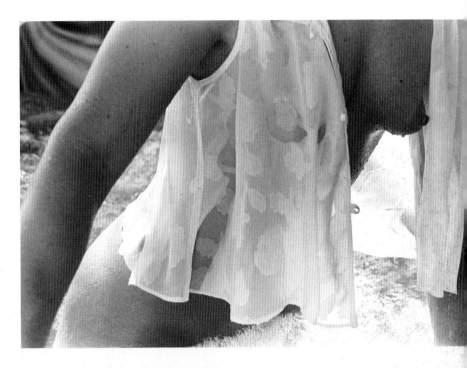

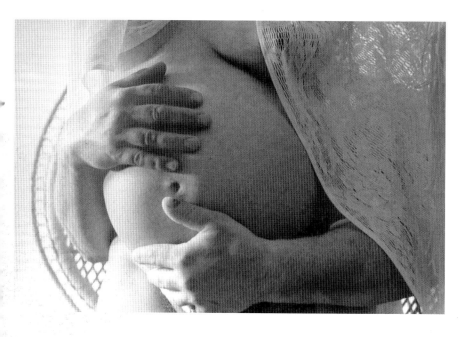

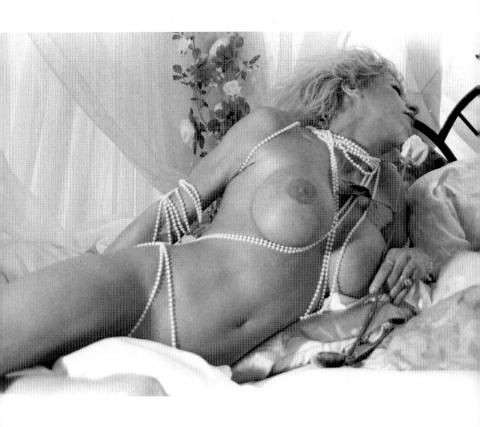

Jozsef Lovasz

Born in Hungary in 1960,
Jozsef Lovasz nurtured a
childhood dream of becoming
a painter. He has long taken a
keen interest in European art,
and is fascinated by the music
of Bela Bartok and Zoltan
Kodaly. His attitude has always
been one of rebellion, and he
actively seeks out controversy.
In Hungary he worked as a
factory worker, waiter and
fashion shop owner. In 1988,
having travelled extensively
throughout Europe, he
emigrated to Australia, where
he is now pursuing his
photographic career.

Jozsef_lo@hotmail.com

MAELWYS

Maelwys is a British artist whose love of art in every form has led him to experiment with many mediums over the years, including photography. As is the case for so many artists, he has a long-standing fascination for the naked human form. The beauty of women, especially placed in a natural environment, has captivated artists since time immemorial, and Maelwys' study of this genre, using many different mediums, has culminated in this collection of images.

www.fetotography.com

JEFFREY MCALLISTER

Jeffrey McAllister has worked
in various areas of the arts for
many years in New England.
In recent years, erotic
photography has compelled Jeff
to explore the power of lust in
art. He says, 'I try to approach
this subject with the same
passion and conviction as one
would approach any subject
worthy of serious study. If an
image of mine can reach inside
a viewer and resonate, and
perhaps touch that person,
reminding him or her that
these things we all crave are
good and real and important,
then I'm happy indeed.'

www.c7erotica.com

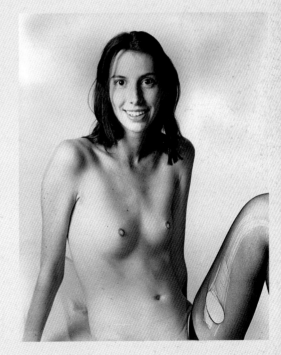

STEPHEN MCCLURE

Stephen McClure was born and raised in Atlanta, Georgia. After high school he went to the small liberal arts college of Kenyon, in Ohio, and as a part of his studies there was required to take art classes in order to become a 'well rounded individual'. This provided his first introduction to photography, and he quickly fell in love with the medium and with making images. He first came to Los Angeles to study photography and 3D computer animation at Art Center College of Design in Pasadena. Major influences in his work come from surrealists, fashion and fetish photographers such as Gilles Berquet, Pierre Molinier, Man Ray, Helmut Newton, Mario Sorrenti and Erwin Olaf.

www.darkenvy.com

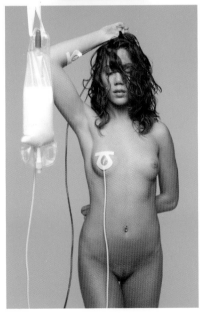

ANDY METAL

Andy Metal was born in 1969 in Toulouse, France, and now lives in Montpellier in the south of France. Since the age of 15 he has processed all his own films, taught by his father, and he still loves classic black and white photography, even though he now uses a computer to do the 'touching up' that was previously done in his photo lab. His main interest is in people. He likes to capture expressions, something special in a face or an attitude – in short, the 'message' of a person or a group. His strongest tributes go to women, who never stop seducing him.

www.andymetal.com

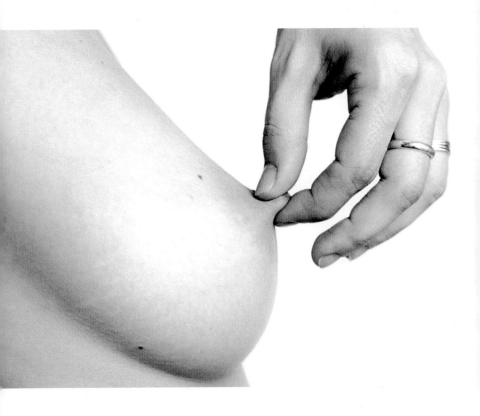

CARINA MEYER-BROICHER

Carina Meyer-Broicher was born in Cologne, Germany, in 1961. She learned to use a camera as a child, and began her professional career as a photographer in the mid 1990s. A colleague once said 'she paints with light', and Carina's photographs, even though they are almost all taken in black and white, show the joy of life. She spent some time living in London, and recently moved back to Germany, where she works as an editor for a photo magazine, as a web designer and as a photographer. Her main photographic interests include the nude, portraits, art and architecture.

www.cologne-photoart.de

LIEVEN MICHIELS

Lieven Michiels is a young audiovisual artist from Brussels, Belgium. He studied architecture in high school and cinematography at the National Radio and Film Institute in Brussels, and then worked as a lighting technician, editor and camera assistant. 'My experience on film sets, dealing with technical issues, has given me the tools to properly express myself,' says Lieven. 'The true masters for me are the master painters such as Rembrandt, Caravaggio and Vermeer. And every day I get a little closer to understanding their story – the story of light.'

http://users.skynet.be/lievenmichiels/ Contact.htm

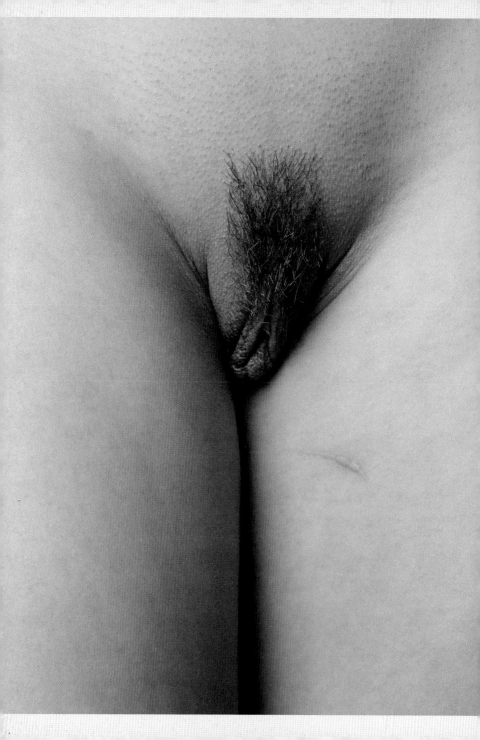

CRAIG MOREY

Craig Morey was born in 1952 in Fort Wayne, Indiana. He attended Indiana University and studied with the noted Bauhaus artist, Henry Holmes Smith. Moving to San Francisco, where he now works, he co-founded the San Francisco Camerawork, which continues to show the most innovative work in contemporary photography. Starting in 1988, on assignment for *Penthouse*, Morey began creating a series of striking black and white nudes, which appeared in numerous publications worldwide. His published books of images include *Studio Nudes* (1992), *Body/Expression/Silence* (1994) and *Linea* (1996). His comprehensive collection, *20th Century Studio Nudes*, was recently published by Glaspalast.

www.moreystudio.com

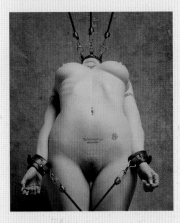

HANS-PETER MUFF

Swiss nude photographer
Hans-Peter Muff lives with his
family in Luzern. His initial
black and white nude
photography, taken during his
four years of teaching, featured
his wife. Since then, he has
worked mainly with models.
His first exhibition was in
1983, at the Nikon gallery in
Zurich, and his film work
(including experimental shorts
*Intermezzo, Einschnitt,
Spiegelbilder, Une Tranche De Vie*
and *Sequenza*) has since been
shown at festivals in Tokyo,
Berlin, Zagreb and
Switzerland. He enjoys
experimenting with all forms
of new techniques and
material. He appeared in the
first volume of *The Mammoth
Book of Erotic Photography*.

www.muff.ch.vu

DAVE NAZ

Dave Naz was born in 1969 in
Los Angeles, California. In his
late teens and early 20s, he
worked as a musician, touring
and putting out records, and in
1995 he picked up the camera
and started photographing
people. He has no formal
training, but his photographs
have now been featured in
numerous publications and
exhibitions around the world. A
collection of Dave's fetish
photographs is featured in the
book *Lust Circus*, published by
Goliath. His second book *Panties*
(Goliath) shows women wearing
no makeup and only cotton
panties. The focus of Dave's
third book, *Legs* (also by
Goliath), is as you would expect.

www.davenaz.com

KIM NIELSEN

Kim Nielsen lives in Jutland, Denmark. In 1999, he decided to learn how to operate a camera, and he taught himself how to capture on film, through the camera lens, the passion that he has for women. The pictures he takes are highly personal, taken because a particular image appeals to him or because it tells a story, an aspect of photography that he believes is important. Kim Nielsen is not a commercial photographer. Photography is his hobby, and the majority of his photoshoots are done on weekends.

www.nudeart.dk

MICHAEL PECHA

Michael Pecha is an Austrian photographer, photo-designer and filmmaker, based in Vienna and Rio de Janeiro. He was born in Vienna in 1966, has worked as an advisor to Leica and has received international awards. He has published 12 books, including *Made In Brasil*, which features Brazilian women. He set up his picture agency at www.foto-production.com, and he works for advertising agencies and magazines, and specialises in photographing people, fashion, lifestyle, erotica, advertising and architecture.

www.pecha-archives.com

ZBIGNIEW RESZKA

Would-be painter Zbigniew Reszka turned to photography to gain a more immediate emotional contact with his subjects, and in the process he has reached a level of intimacy that his models sometimes find too close for comfort. 'Some models look at the pictures and find them terrifying. Others recognise themselves in ways that go far beyond the poses and the acts themselves.'

Reszka often adds dimension to the negatives by scratching in comments, highlights and symbols. His works are in private collections in Germany, France, England, Switzerland, the Netherlands, Finland and Japan. His public exhibitions have included the Polish Council in Rome (1996) and Paris (1997).

www.spirala.prv.pl

GABRIELE RIGON

Gabriele Rigon is an Italian
photographer who previously
worked as a helicopter pilot for
the United Nations forces in
Lebanon. His passion is for
portrait and fine art nude
photography, and he has
quickly established himself as
one of the more prominent
and luminous artists in the
field, with a book from Diverse
Publications (2004), and a wide
range of magazine and book
cover appearances (including
various editions of the
notorious book by Italian
schoolgirl Melissa P). He
appeared in the first volume of
*The Mammoth Book Of Erotic
Photography*.

www.gabrielerigon.it

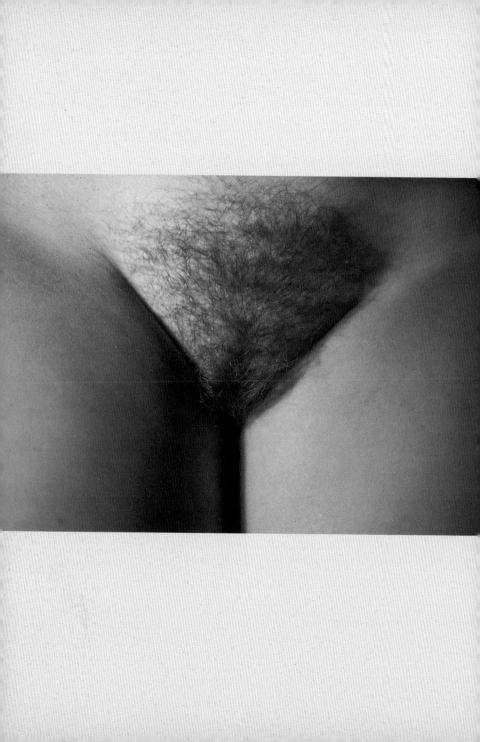

Juan Carlos Rivas

Born in 1958, in Arenas de San Pedro, Spain, Juan Carlos Rivas now lives and works in Madrid, where he contributes to a cinema magazine for Spanish public television and writes movie reviews. Cinema influences his photographic vision, and many of his pictures reveal a sense of *mise en scene*. He adores hotel beds, windows, empty rooms, big clear spaces – places where you can imagine something happening before and after the image was taken. 'I'm always searching for the erotic state of mind that looking at a naked woman engenders. For that reason, I always work with the light I find on the scene, never studio, never flash.'

www.juancarlosrivas.com

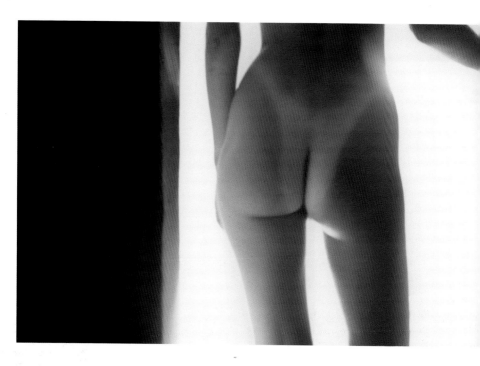

KATI RUDLOVA

Kati Rudlova was born in Ostrava, an industrial town in the Czech Republic. She began to take photographs when she was 12 years old, after her parents gave her first camera, and photography became her passion. She has now explored this world both as a model and as a photographer. Since first posing as a model in 1998, she has had the opportunity to work with many photographers, and she appears in this book in three separate portfolios.

In 2002, she bought a Canon EOS 5, once again took up her position behind the camera, and began to take photographs of herself.

www.katirudlova.com

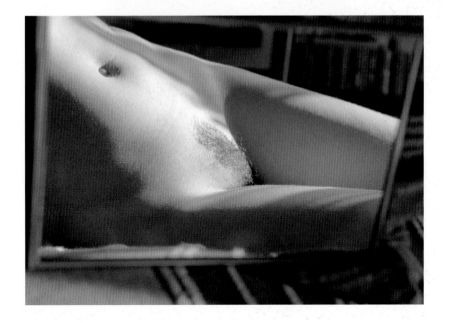

JOHN RUNNING

John Running has lived in Flagstaff, Arizona, for the past 35 years, and has been taking photographs for advertising, design and editorial clients for nearly 30 years. Running has been photographing the female nude throughout his career. He specialises in photographing people on location or in the studio, and his photographs stand out because they have a style that is personally creative and graphically strong. The women he photographs are both sensual and strong, and he sees his images as collaborations with his models in which both parties can express their creativity.

www.johnrunning.com

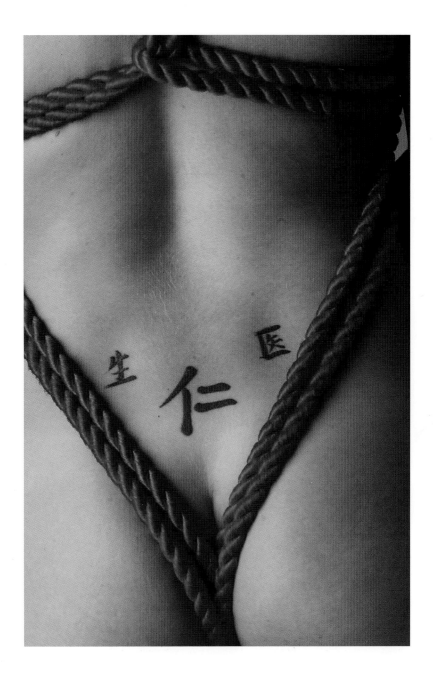

RAECHEL RUNNING

Raechel Marie Running's lifetime passion for photography began when she picked up the camera at the age of 15. 'My task as a photographer is to create a space between myself and the sitter, and invite the muse. We explore and discover the many parts of ourselves through creative play. Each woman holds within her the mystery and beauty of the ages. It's a dance of masks: mystery; beauty; love; dreams.' Her work is a hybrid of traditional photography personally touched with hand colouring, collage and digital imaging. Raechel shares a studio with her father and colleague John Running in Flagstaff, Arizona.

www.RMRunningFOTO.com

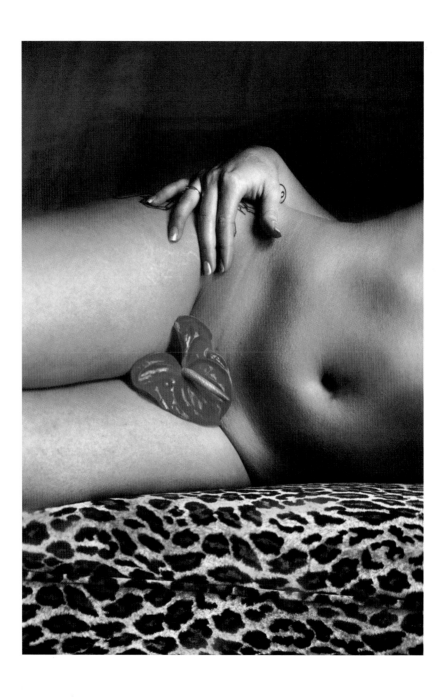

WILL SANTILLO

Will Santillo began his studies of photography while at Massachusetts Institute of Technology (MIT), studying under master photographer Minor White and obtaining a degree in Art and Design. He continued his education at the University of Toronto, receiving a professional degree in architecture. In his long career as a photographer, he has worked in a variety of fields, including fashion, corporate, architectural, personal and intimate portraiture. He has been published in several major North American consumer and professional publications, and has participated in group shows in New York, Berlin and Toronto. His work has also been featured in a one-man show in Toronto and on television.

www.santillophotography.com

IVAN SCHEERS

Ivan Scheers was born in 1962 and lives in Belgium. Buying his first reflex camera at the age of 18, he considered studying photography in order to follow a career as a professional photographer, but is glad he didn't, as his photography now arises purely out of passion for the medium. His creativity is not limited by the need to satisfy customers, and he can pursue his own ideas and visions. Ivan nearly always works with inexperienced models, striving to capture the curves of naked bodies and the texture of their skin.

www.ivanscheers.com

MATT SCHNEIDER

Matthew Schneider is based in
Portland, Oregon. The Pacific
Northwest provides a rich and
varied environment for his
photography, with its coastline
and mountains, lakes and
waterfalls, nude beaches and
hot springs. Although a
computer programmer by
occupation, he has avoided
digital photography in favour
of black and white film and a
medium format camera. His
work has been published in
several books and magazines,
and his large format prints can
be seen hanging in Portland art
galleries.

www.ms-photo.com

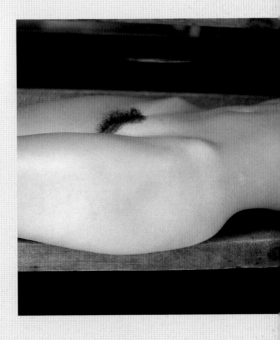

IAN SCRIVENER

Ian Scrivener was born in 1965 and lives at Bondi Beach, in Sydney Australia. His passion for, and involvement in, art nude photography stretches back over 20 years. He strives to find a real connection with the model, to reveal some of the private person, not just the beautiful form. He shows women comfortable and empowered. He prefers to shoot on location outdoors, which can be challenging in the harsh Australian sun. Most of his locations are amongst Australia's rugged rocky landscapes or in abandoned stone buildings. He is fascinated by the contrast between old, decaying stone and new flesh.

www.ianscrivener.com

MICHELE SERCHUK

Michele Serchuk is currently a Photography Associate for *On Our Backs* magazine and is regularly published there, in *Cupido,* and in many other fetish and erotica magazines, as well as in books and as cover art in the US and England. She has exhibited in galleries around the US, and appeared on local NYC TV shows. Her models all share the desire to take erotic exploration into a visual realm. In her work, Serchuk prefers to follow her models' passions rather than casting them as people they are not. They are active participants in the orchestration of the images, as they reveal to us their own personal fascinations, fetishes and fantasies.

www.photodiva.com
www.micheleserchuk.com

JUERGEN SPECHT

To German photographer Juergen Specht, women are beautiful and light is fascinating. Specht uses the beauty of a woman to play with light, allowing her natural form to create an installation that is less about the erotic than about the expression of his own visual thinking. This expression is the consuming passion of his life. 'Ideas come to me,' he says, 'demanding realisation. They take up space in my mind, growing larger and larger until there is nothing I can do but get them out of my mind into photographs, freeing me to move on.' Juergen is currently living in Tokyo.

www.juergenspecht.com

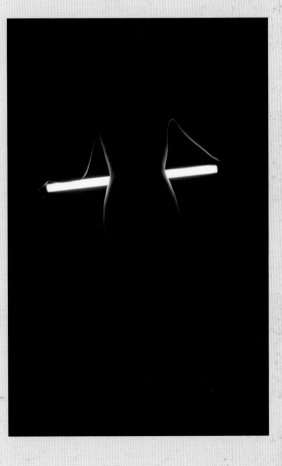

JOERN STUBBE

Joern Stubbe was born in 1976 in Blankenburg, Germany, and began working in photography in 1999. He now lives in Leipzig. His preferred genre is fine art nude photography. On the basis that less is more, Stubbe works only in black and white and likes to present his models in a natural way, allowing the viewer to concentrate on shape and contrast. For his sessions, he prefers spontaneity, often letting himself be inspired by the location, so that every picture feels different from shoot to shoot.

www.js-fotografie.de

MARCO TENAGLIA

Italian professional
photographer Marco Tenaglia
was born in 1971 in Rome,
and has specialised in fashion,
beauty and modelling
photography. Having worked in
both Europe and the US, he
feels he has now combined
European elegance with
American style to create a new
and unique kind of
photography through which he
can express himself. 'I'm a
dreamer,' he says, 'and all of my
life is a dream. At this point in
my artistic career I have
somehow discovered a fantastic
way to express the atmosphere
of my dreams. This is it.'

www.marcotenaglia.com

CARSTEN TSCHACH

After spending time working on landscape and travel photography, Carsten Tschach found he needed a new challenge, and moved – almost unintentionally – into erotic art photography. The purpose of his images is to attract the viewer and arouse the imagination. 'It's not just a question of nudity – it's the play of light and shadows that sometimes makes the models take on a mystical aura and allows the onlooker to create his own fantasy.' He has recently created images for the cosmetic industry and has, as a result, extended his activities into more commercial areas. He lives and works in Berlin, Germany.

www.sensual-eye.com

MIKKEL URUP

Mikkel Urup was born in Charlottenlund, Denmark. In 1986, he enjoyed his first public individual exhibition of photos and paintings. Educated as an airbrush artist, he later took a course in artistic working methods in Florida. From 1990 to 1995 he worked as an advertising director, meanwhile establishing himself as a recognised photographer. In 1996, his paintings were accepted by 'Den Fri', a prestigious group exhibition in Denmark. Since then, in addition to his photographic work, he has made several acclaimed short films and two feature films.

www.profilfoto.dk

LARRY UTLEY

Larry Utley is a San Francisco-
based photographer and artist.
His interest in photographing
the BDSM scene began some
years ago when he first
attended San Francisco's
hyperbolic Folsom Street Fair.
He has photographed an
extraordinary range of
professional dom and sub
enthusiasts ever since. Utley's
most recent book *Women In
Control: Iron Fist, Velvet Glove*
continues his photographic
anthology of female
dominance, power and control.
Previously published works
include *Fetish Fashion:
Undressing The Corset* and
showcases at exhibitions in San
Francisco, New York and
London.

www.larryutley.com

MARIANO VARGAS

Mariano Vargas is a Spanish photographer who works and lives in Marbella. A selection of his erotic photographs have been published in a book entitled *Pxotos*. In his highly distinctive and wittily computer-modified images, Mariano places gorgeous creatures in surreal surroundings to produce 'the ultimate in heavenly fantasies'. He won the Erotic Award for Best Photographer of the Year in 2003.

www.lasagradavulva.com

KIM WESTON

A third-generation member of one of the most important and creative families in photography, Kim Weston has been a fine art photographer for almost 30 years. Kim creates his own photographs using innovative sets that he designs and constructs in his studio at Wildcat Hill in California, the former home of Kim's grandfather, Edward Weston. He also shares his passion, artistry and unique photographic vision with his wife, Gina. Together they teach select groups of participants at workshops. Kim has had numerous exhibitions of his work throughout the US and Europe.

www.kimweston.com

RENÉ WHITFIELD

René Whitfield is a 32-year-old Danish photographer who lives in Copenhagen with his wife and son. After a 15-year break from his greatest interest, photography, in 2001 he became greatly inspired by Petter Hegre, picked up his camera and began taking pictures of his wife. These images were well received, were published in several magazines and even won him a 'photographer of the year' award. He now he uses his time for private commissions, and does model tests for agencies. He still can't make up his mind between fashion and erotic images, but he does know that it needs to be personal.

www.renewhitfield.dk

MICHAEL WILCE

Michael Wilce is based in London and has been working in photography since 1989. He started on a local newspaper, and then freelanced as a press photographer, a black and white printer, an assistant for a few fashion/portrait/advertising photographers and occasionally as a model. He started photographing nudes almost by accident. A small literary magazine that had used some of his press photos asked if he could do a photo for the cover and so – 'what the hell' – he did a naked self portrait. People saw it and asked if he could photograph them.

www.mikesphotos.ukf.net

JAMES WILLIAMS

James Williams was born and raised in Las Vegas, Nevada. A father of three, he uses his wife as model in most of his images. He first picked up on the beauty of the female form in *Playboy*, and never imagined that one day he'd be shooting nudes himself. Over recent years he has changed the vision of what he wants to shoot and has turned to more artistic work rather than glamour. His inspirations include Helmut Newton, Mapplethorpe, Demarchelier and various web-based photographers, such as Lindsay Garrett, Gennadi and Rob Debenport.

www.beauty-nudes.com
www.jwilliams-photography.com

ABOUT THE EDITOR

MAXIM JAKUBOWSKI is the editor of the best-selling *Mammoth Book of Erotica* series, now into its tenth volume, as well as *The Mammoth Book of Erotic Online Diaries*. A columnist for *The Guardian*, novelist and broadcaster, he lives in London, where he owns the world-famous Murder One bookshop.